This Bing book belongs to:

..........................

Copyright © 2016 Acamar Films Ltd

First published in the UK in 2016 by HarperCollins *Children's Books,*
a division of HarperCollins *Publishers* Ltd, 1 London Bridge Street, London SE1 9GF.
This edition published by HarperCollins *Children's Books* in 2018.

3 5 7 9 10 8 6 4 2

ISBN: 978-0-00-797696-6

Based on the script by Lead Writer: Lizzie Ennever and Team Writers:
Lucy Murphy, Ted Dewan, Mikael Shields and Philip Bergkvist

Adapted from the original books by Ted Dewan and using images created by Acamar Films and Brown Bag Films

Edited by Neil Dunnicliffe, Freddie Hutchins and An Vrombaut

Designed by Rachel Lawston

Printed in China .

# Dressing Up

HarperCollins *Children's Books*

Round the corner,
not far away, Bing is
dressing up today.

Bing, Coco and Flop are **dancing** around Bing's bedroom.

Da-ka, da-ka, do-doh...

Da-ka, da-ka, do-doh!

"Oh, I love
dressing up!"
says Coco.

"Me too!"
replies Bing.

Bing and Coco both reach into the box.
They're in such a **hurry** that they **bang** heads.

*OUCH!*

Flop gives their heads a little rub. "Well, there are **two** of you and only **one** box, so what do we do now?"

"Let's take turns," says Coco. "I'm first."

Coco dives into the box and pulls out a **twirly tutu.** She **swishes** around the room.

"I'm a **princess...** Princess Coco-ca-pono. And you can be **King Bing.**"

"OK!" says Bing. "My turn."
He pulls out his shiny armour.

"Aha! I'm **King** Bing!"

Flop finds a hat with **jingly** bells on.

"And I'll be the Royal Dresser-upper," he says.

It's Coco's turn again. She picks a **sparkly necklace**. "Aha! Princess Coco-ca-pono's jewels!"

Bing chooses his **superhero belt**
and ZOOMS around the room.

**"Neeeeeeeooooooooowwwwwww!"**

"I'm a **Super** King!"

"A superhero belt's not very kingy, Bing,"
frowns Coco.

Next, Coco chooses a **gold bag.**

"Perfectly princessy! Your turn, Bing."

Bing ZOOMS over to the box and
pulls out a fuzzy lion tail.

"Ha-ha! I'm Super **Lion** King Bing!
King of ALL the animals!"

"A tail?" says Coco.
"That's not even a BIT kingy."

But Bing isn't listening. He dives back into the box and pulls out a **magic wand.**

**"And now, Super Lion King Bing is magic!"**

"You can't be magic and a Super Lion King," says Coco.

"Anyway, you're not even a proper king. Look – you haven't got a crown!"

"I **have** got a **crown**," says Bing.
"See – it's here, in my dressing up box!"

# "I'm Super Magic Lion King Bing!"

"No, Bing. I'M the princess – I need the crown!" says Coco, and she snatches it from Bing's head.

# "See? I'm Princess Coco-ca-pono!"

"Taking a king's crown isn't very **princessy**, Coco," says Flop.

"Hey!" says Bing. "I had the crown first."
And he snatches it back.

"Taking the crown back isn't
very kingy, Bing," says Flop.
"There are two of you and
only one crown, so what
do we do now?"

Bing and Coco both grab hold of the crown.
"Give it back!" they shout.

"Careful," warns Flop...

Snap

"**Oh no!**
Now there's
NO crown at all,"
says Coco.

"It's all broken,
Flop!" cries Bing.

"Things can **break** if you fight over them," says Flop. He picks up a jewel from the floor.

"Well, there are **two** of you, and **lots of jewels**. Let's see what we can do. May I borrow your magic wand, King Bing?"

Flop fetches a piece of **gold card** and some **glue**. He **taps** the card with the wand. "Glue here, please, King Bing."

Bing **blobs** glue onto the card.
"And jewels on top," says Flop.

"That's **not** a crown!" says Coco.

"Not yet..." says Flop.

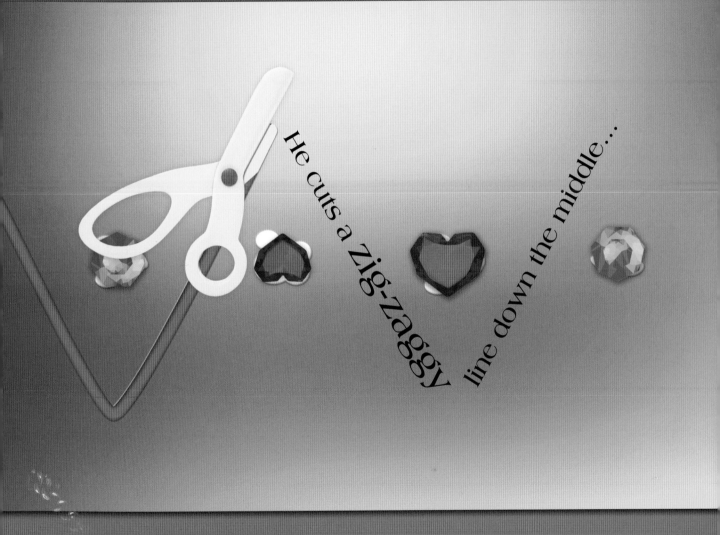

He cuts a zig-zaggy line down the middle...

...and bends the two pieces.

Flop has made **TWO** crowns!

# "Aha!

## I've got a crown again!" shouts Bing.

"And me!" laughs Coco. "I'm Princess Coco-ca-pono again!"

"Thank you, Royal Dresser-upper Flop," says Bing. "Now I'm Super Magic Lion King Bing of **everything!**"

Good for you, Bing Bunny.

**Hi!**

Me and Coco and Flop played **dressing up**, and I was King Bing.

But there was only **one crown**, and Princess Coco-ca-pono wanted it too.

So we pulled it and it went

# SNAP

and it broke.

We both **felt bad**, but Flop showed us how to share the jewels to make **two new crowns**.

And I was **Super Magic Lion King Bing** again!

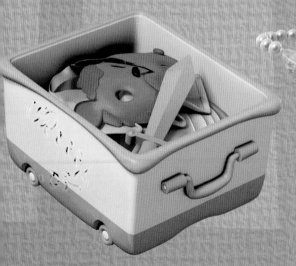

When you **fight** over something it can **break**, but if you **share** the jewels you can both have a crown.

Dressing up...

it's a Bing thing.